Pebble®

Dogs

Gre🐾t Danes

by Connie Colwell Miller

Consulting Editor: Gail Saunders-Smith, PhD

Consultant: Jennifer Zablotny, DVM
Member, American Veterinary Medical Association

Capstone
press®

Mankato, Minnesota

Pebble Books are published by Capstone Press,
151 Good Counsel Drive, P.O. Box 669, Mankato, Minnesota 56002.
www.capstonepress.com

1 2 3 4 5 6 12 11 10 09 08 07

Library of Congress Cataloging-in-Publication Data
Miller, Connie Colwell, 1976–
    Great danes / by Connie Colwell Miller.
    p. cm.—(Pebble Books. Dogs.)
    Summary: "Simple text and photographs present the great dane breed and how
to care for them"—Provided by publisher.
    Includes bibliographical references and index.
    ISBN-13: 978-0-7368-6742-9 (hardcover)
    ISBN-10: 0-7368-6742-2 (hardcover)
    1. Great Dane—Juvenile literature. I. Title. II. Series.
SF429.G7M53 2007
636.73—dc22   2006026567

Note to Parents and Teachers

The Dogs set supports national science standards related to life
science. This book describes and illustrates Great Danes. The images
support early readers in understanding the text. The repetition of
words and phrases helps early readers learn new words. This book
also introduces early readers to subject-specific vocabulary words,
which are defined in the Glossary section. Early readers may need
assistance to read some words and to use the Table of Contents,
Glossary, Read More, Internet Sites, and Index sections of the book.

Table of Contents

The Gentle Giant

The Great Dane is one
of the tallest dog breeds
in the world.
Full-grown Great Danes
are as tall as ponies.

Great Danes are large.
But they are not clumsy.
They are gentle
and graceful dogs.

From Puppy to Adult

Great Dane puppies
are bigger and heavier
than some adult dogs
of other breeds.

Young Great Danes
need lots of training.
Large dogs must behave
well so they don't hurt
people by accident.

Full-grown Great Danes are larger than most dogs. They need larger leashes and bigger toys.

Great Dane Care

Great Danes need lots of food and water. They eat about 8 cups of dog food every day.

Great Danes enjoy resting indoors with their owners. They need daily walks. They are unhappy when left alone in kennels.

Great Danes have
short coats.
Owners should brush their
dogs once each week.

Great Danes are big dogs that make great pets. Owners love these gentle giants.

Glossary

behave—to act properly

breed—a certain kind of animal within an animal group

clumsy—careless and awkward in your movements

coat—a dog's fur

gentle—not rough

giant—a very large and strong creature

graceful—able to move quickly and easily

kennel—an outside cage where a dog is kept

train—to teach an animal how to do something

Read More

Murray, Julie. *Great Danes.* Dogs. Edina, Minn.: Abdo, 2003.

Preszler, June. *Caring for Your Dog.* First Facts: Positively Pets. Mankato, Minn.: Capstone, 2007.

Internet Sites

FactHound offers a safe, fun way to find Internet sites related to this book. All of the sites on FactHound have been researched by our staff.

Here's how:

1. Visit *www.facthound.com*

2. Choose your grade level.

3. Type in this book ID **0736867422** for age-appropriate sites. You may also browse subjects by clicking on letters, or by clicking on pictures and words.

4. Click on the **Fetch It** button.

FactHound will fetch the best sites for you!   23

Index

Word Count: 149
Grade: 1
Early-Intervention Level: 14

Editorial Credits
Martha E. H. Rustad, editor; Juliette Peters, set designer; Kyle Grenz, book designer; Kara Birr, photo researcher; Scott Thoms, photo editor

Photo Credits
Bruce Coleman Inc./Jean Claude Carton, cover; Capstone Press/Karon Dubke, 14, 16, 18; Corbis/Deanne Fitzmaurice, 4; Getty Images Inc./Taxi/Mel Yates, 20; Getty Images Inc./The Image Bank/GK Hart/Vikki Hart, 10; Mark Raycroft, 6, 8; UNICORN Stock Photos/Rod Furgason, 12; www.jeanmfogle.com, 1